FIFE COUNCIL LIBRARIES
FC083463
KT-584-398

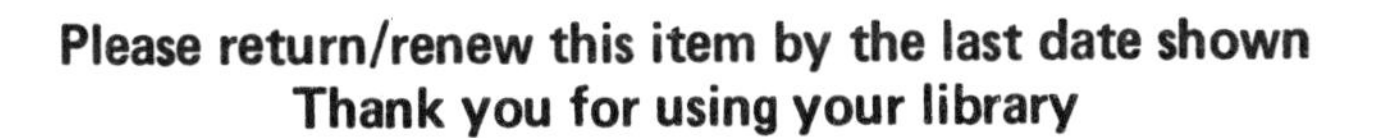

Please return/renew this item by the last date shown
Thank you for using your library

FIFE COUNCIL LIBRARIES

PUFFIN BOOKS

CHILLERS

The Blob Tessa Potter and Peter Cottrill
Clive and the Missing Finger Sarah Garland
The Day Matt Sold Great-grandma Eleanor Allen and Jane Cope
The Dinner Lady Tessa Potter and Karen Donelly
Ghost from the Sea Eleanor Allen and Leanne Franson
Hide and Shriek! Paul Dowling
Jimmy Woods and the Big Bad Wolf Mick Gowar and Barry Wilkinson
Madam Sizzers Sarah Garland
The Real Porky Philips Mark Haddon
Sarah Scarer Sally Christie and Claudio Muñoz
Spooked Philip Wooderson and Jane Cope
Wilf the Black Hole Hiawyn Oram and Dee Shulman

PUFFIN BOOKS

Published by the Penguin Group
Penguin Books Ltd, 27 Wrights Lane, London W8 5TZ, England
Penguin Books USA Inc., 375 Hudson Street, New York, New York 10014, USA
Penguin Books Australia Ltd, Ringwood, Victoria, Australia
Penguin Books Canada Ltd, 10 Alcorn Avenue, Toronto, Ontario, Canada M4V 3B2
Penguin Books (NZ) Ltd, 182–190 Wairau Road, Auckland 10, New Zealand

Penguin Books Ltd, Registered Offices: Harmondsworth, Middlesex, England

First published by A&C Black (Publishers) Ltd 1994
Published in Puffin Books 1996
3 5 7 9 10 8 6 4

Copyright © Sarah Garland, 1994
All rights reserved

The moral right of the author/illustrator has been asserted

Filmset in Meridien

Made and printed in England by William Clowes Ltd, Beccles and London

Except in the United States of America, this book is sold subject to the condition that it shall not, by way of trade or otherwise, be lent, re-sold, hired out, or otherwise circulated without the publisher's prior consent in any form of binding or cover other than that in which it is published and without a similar condition including this condition being imposed on the subsequent purchaser

Madam Sizzers walked the streets of Marrakesh in heavy disguise.

Her partner, Trice, walked a few steps behind her, carrying a metal strongbox. His eyes darted anxiously from side to side. Beneath his light jacket nestled a large revolver.

Chapter One

Rachel Morgan and Lola Delaney were best friends. But sometimes they had what Rachel's mum called "a bit of a ding-dong".

They were having one that day under the cheese plant in the hairdresser's.

"That's not a poem," said Lola scornfully.

"Tell me yours then, if it's so brilliant," said Rachel.

"All right," said Lola and she began,

The Cat by Lola Delaney
Eyes like ~~torches~~ headlamps
Burning bright
In the ~~jungles~~ forests
Of the night
~~What is awful,~~
What the

"Hang on. That sounds sort of familiar," said Rachel doubtfully.

Lola jumped to her feet in a rage and hit her head on a shelf of shampoos.

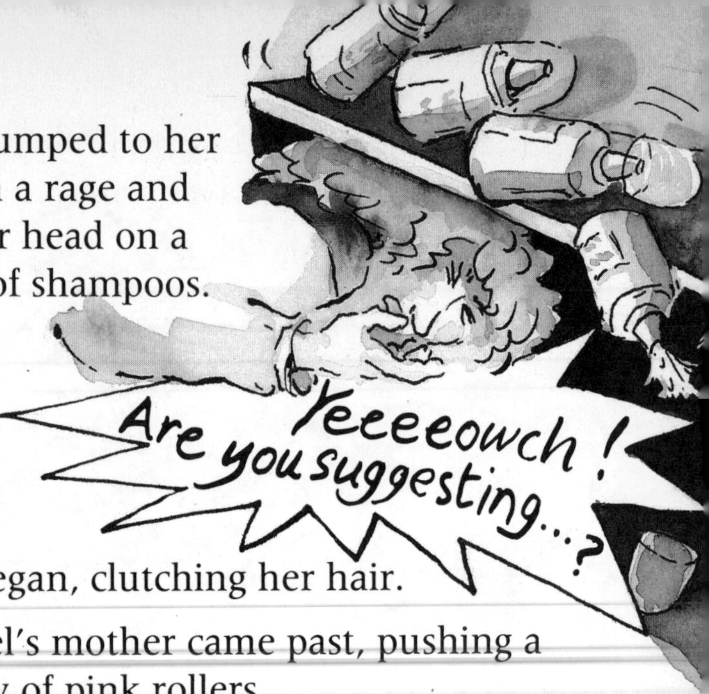

Yeeeeowch!

Are you suggesting...?

she began, clutching her hair.

Rachel's mother came past, pushing a trolley of pink rollers.

She paused and rubbed Lola's head, then bent down and peered into her face.

What a MESS!

"Let me cut your fringe, Lola. I can hardly see your eyes any more."

"Never ever!" said Rachel and Lola together.

"Well no more ding-dongs then," sighed Rachel's mother, as she went on to finish Mrs Dougall's perm.

Lola screwed up her poem and threw it in the bin.

"I'm bored with poetry. Let's go out."

They stood in the doorway and looked down the street. The signboard on the pavement groaned uneasily in the wind.

"She's coming back from her holidays tomorrow, Madam Sizzers is," said Rachel gloomily. "It won't be fun here any more, like it is with Mum. And I can't go to Gran's now she's in hospital."

"And my house isn't much good. Too many babies," said Lola.

At that moment a huge red motorbike raced down the street towards them, and braked so hard that the tyres screeched and smoked against the kerb.

The driver pushed up his visor, took a packet from his pouch and beckoned to Rachel and Lola.

"Delivery from Premier Couriers for Salon Sizzers. Take it in for me, there's good girls. Special delivery for a lucky lady."

Rachel brightened immediately.

"Right on," said the man, throwing his bike into gear and roaring away up the hill.

Rachel and Lola sat on the steps of the War Memorial and untied the string.

"Lucky Lady. Isn't that what you sent off for ages ago? The present you ordered for your mum?" asked Lola.

"Yep," said Rachel, pulling at the sticky tape with her teeth.

Inside the box was another parcel of thick, waxed paper and inside that, a little leather pouch. Rachel pulled the drawstrings apart and tipped it upside down.

"That's odd!" she said.

A jumble of rough, heavy stones rolled out on to the step.

"What did you order in the end? Was it Glints of Fire?" asked Lola.

"No. Sea Foam. I thought it would go with Mum's blue dress. But these are a bit dark.

A Lucky Lady necklace for that very special gift," she murmured. "That's what it said in the advertisement. These aren't even joined up."

But Lola was impressed. She held a stone up against the sky and squinted at the rich green light that gleamed from deep inside it.

"Like sunbeams in a rock pool. Your mum'll love these," she said. "It's real quality. I might start saving up for some. Sixty-five pence wasn't it?"

"Seventy-five. But it was a special offer. They might have gone up. Let's go and get some elastic and make them into a proper necklace."

Rachel stuffed the pouch of beads into her jeans pocket, where they rubbed uncomfortably as she ran across to the shops.

The narrow beam of a torch wavered across the floor of the salon.

Madam Sizzers pulled down the blinds before switching on the desk lamp.

''You blithering fool, Trice,'' she spat out. ''What possessed you to change the courier? If this trip goes wrong you're for it. Geddit? Finito!''

Trice blanched. ''It seemed a good idea at the time,'' he muttered, pulling nervously at his moustache.

Chapter Two

Madam Sizzers twisted restlessly in the high-backed chair behind the reception desk (her throne, Lola called it). She drummed her long sharp nails on the leather appointment book.

"I haven't much choice have I, Lynette? You have to look after your clients, so I'll have these infants under my feet all day."

She threw a withering glance at Rachel and Lola.

"Thank you. I'll make sure they behave well," said Rachel's mother.

"How dignified Mum is," thought Rachel. "I could *kill* Madam Sizzers. Snip her into little bits. She knows no one would have their hair done here if it weren't for Mum."

She and Lola trailed off to the waiting area and settled on the wicker sofa under an aspidistra.

"What shall we do, Lola?"

"I'm going to write a poem of hate," said Lola briskly, taking her exercise book out of a plastic bag. "I've thrown away the cat poem. I think I might have sort of heard it before, like distant cheering at a football match, or a radio playing three gardens away on a summer's afternoon."

"Oh heavens, Lola!" said Rachel in an irritated voice. "Can't you just talk straight? Everything doesn't *have* to be like something else *all* the time."

"It does if you are training to be a poet," said Lola.

"What's so marvellous about being a poet anyway?" muttered Rachel, feeling gloomier than ever.

She slumped down in her chair, thrusting her hands deep into her pockets to feel the nice, knobbly shapes of the green beads, now strung into a necklace. Her eyes were half shut as she imagined her mum unfolding pink tissue paper on her birthday next Sunday, and lifting the gleaming necklace to her throat.

She was so lost in this dream that she didn't notice Madam Sizzers tapping her desk in frustration as she made endless phone calls to Marrakesh.

"Put me through at once! Speak up man! Yes, Premier Couriers Worldwide! You've never heard of them? I'm speaking from England, ENGLAND."

Rachel didn't see her striding the salon, or hear her sharp remarks to clients.

A nice blue rinse might help camouflage the ears Mrs Pierce.

A little more height at the crown would add an element of surprise, certainly.

Don't ask me dear. I would have given up long ago.

"How jumpy everyone is," thought Rachel, opening her eyes. An old lady sat nervously under the drier, her hands so shaky that she finally spilled her coffee into her lap. Rachel watched the anxious sideways glances of the hair-washing boy, as he scalded the mayor's head with the spray.

"It's never like this when Mum's here on her own," she thought.

"Oh my God, the last straw!" hissed Madam Sizzers, as the door was blocked, the salon darkened, and wails arose from four little throats.

Lola's mother was struggling to force her way through the entrance, a baby strapped to her bosom and a double pushchair of twins jammed sideways in the doorway.

The toddler was already inside, advancing across the pale carpet, dripping red jam from a doughnut.

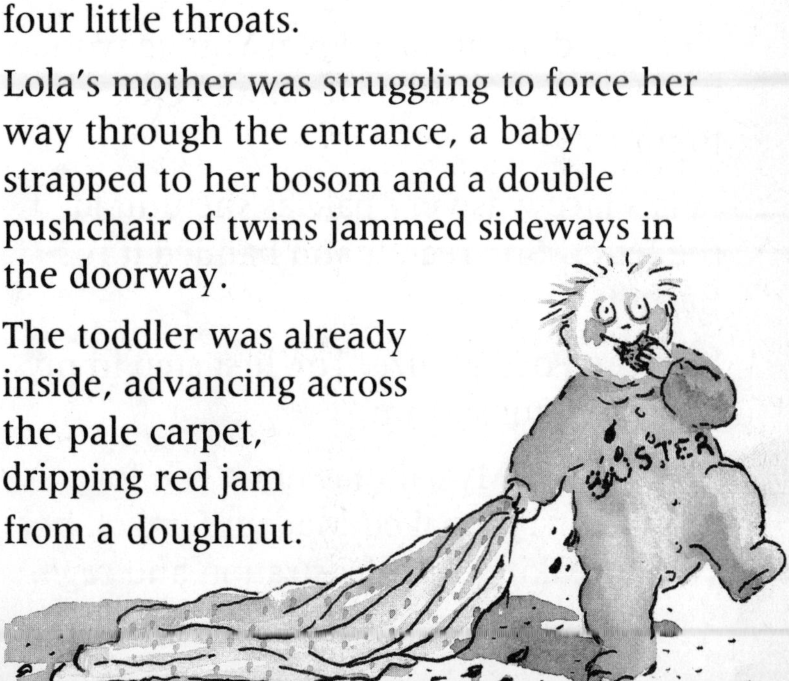

Lola's mother finally managed to climb over the pushchair. She ran across the salon, tripping on a rubber plant and falling on her knees by the sofa.

"You've done it Lola, love! You've won it! Look! You're to be on Blue Peter tomorrow!"

Lola's face was very pale as she unfolded the letter. She read it and handed it to Rachel.

"It's the Poetry Prize. The first step in my career. Thanks Mum."

"Out! OUT! My salon is not a zoo for filthy brats!" croaked Madam Sizzers, her voice breaking with frustration and rage.

Lola's mum collected her babies and stalked out, followed by Rachel and Lola.

"Aren't you excited? Isn't it fabulous?" cried Rachel.

Lola stopped and turned a stricken face towards her.

"But I've got nothing to *wear* on telly," she groaned.

"You can borrow my best party dress if you want. And how about the Lucky Lady necklace?" said Rachel.

Lola's face cleared.

''Creeeow! Creeeow!'' howled Madam Sizzers' Siamese cat.

''There, there, my angelkins,'' crooned Sizzers, setting a dish of poached salmon heads on the floor.

''Turn on the news Trice, you great oaf. No sign of the stones, of course. Your Premier Courier must be feeling very pleased with himself: those gems will set him up for life. Wait! My God! What's that girl wearing? It's that little trollop friend of what's-her-name. And look! See what's round her neck!''

''The flipping emeralds!'' breathed Trice.

Chapter Three

"We'll be too late!" wailed Rachel, stamping with impatience outside the door of their flat.

"Key, key!" muttered her mother, finally emptying her bag upside down on the pavement.

Rachel pounced, and was through the door and in front of the television in a flash.

And there was Lola, standing bravely in a circle of light, reading the last verse of her poem. The Blue Peter team, complete with cats and dogs, were sitting on boxes around her.

"What a dream!" sighed Rachel.

"Yes, doesn't she look lovely," said her mum. "Your dress does suit her, and what a pretty necklace."

"Tell the viewers, Lola," said the Blue Peter presenter, "what you want to be when you grow up."

Lola threw her a withering glance.

"What do you think? A bank robber? Oh. Sorry . . ." she pulled herself together. "No, I'd like to be a poet," she added lamely.

"And now, on to our exciting hydro-electric project up the Ganges," said the presenter quickly, as the screen filled with thundering waterfalls.

Rachel lay back on the sofa, breathing heavily. "Crumbs! Wasn't she fantastic! No one would guess she'd been sick in the ladies' toilets three times this morning."

Rachel's mother eased off her shoes and looked at her swollen red feet.

"A new bunion. Oh dear," she said.

"I wish you didn't have to work for horrible Sizzers," said Rachel.

"Ho-hum. Not so easy to find jobs these days," sighed her mum. "I'm lucky really."

They ate salmon paste sandwiches and watched the News.

"Bunion.
Onion.
Funny one.
'Put a funny
Onion
On your
Bunion."
It's no
good. I'm
useless at
poems.

The next day, Rachel and Lola met on the corner and set off for the hospital, carrying a box of chocolates for Rachel's gran.

Lola didn't talk much about her television appearance. She just said it had been "as hot as Hades" and that she "couldn't remember much, really".

"Something much more exciting happened last night," said Lola at last. "Dad foiled a burglar!"

"What?"

"He was up with one of the twins and heard a noise in the larder.

When he opened the door he saw a horrible arm with long red nails dangling in through the little window, sort of scrabbling about.

He dumped the
twin and grabbed
at the arm,
but it wrenched
itself free and
slithered off.

And then the coal
bunker crashed
outside, and the
gate banged, and
then it was all
quiet. Quiet as a
boneyard."

They had reached the hospital and began to slide down the long, green, polished corridors. There was no one about except for two nurses in the distance, clothed entirely in green from head to toe, with only their eyes showing.

"I might as well give you back the Lucky Lady necklace while I remember," panted Lola as they rested against the wall. She fished in her pocket.

"Thanks," said Rachel. Then her voice rose to a shriek. "LOLA! LOLA!"

A huge trolley thundered towards them with the nurses behind it, their eyes intent and flashing above their masks. Rachel and Lola were pinned against the wall, winded, breathless, trying to shout

. . . to scream . . .

The taller nurse hurled herself

across the trolley,

grunting, reaching for the

necklace. With . . .

hands dipped in blood!

thought Rachel

for a horrible moment.

No, it's nail polish

. . . help! . . . I can't breathe.

She gripped

the necklace fiercely.

''*What* is going on?''
demanded a sharp
voice.

''Sorry matron,'' growled the short nurse hoarsely. They sped away up the corridor, leaving the trolley to glide on and knock the outraged matron in the stomach.

''Appalling behaviour!'' she stuttered, and pounded after the nurses in her sensible shoes.

Rachel and Lola blinked at each other.

Then Lola climbed heavily on to the trolley and lay down.

"You can push me the rest of the way. I've had a very nasty shock."

"So have I. We'll take turns," said Rachel, grimly.

As she pushed, she noticed a little heap of earth that trickled from the trolley and scattered behind them along the polished floor.

Rachel's granny thought the girls were unnaturally quiet. She felt quite anxious about their health, and insisted that they eat all the chocolates, which they did.

Inside a van in the car park, Sizzers and Trice were struggling out of their stiff, starched clothes.

"What a wash-out," said Madam Sizzers. "Lucky that matron was such a cissy. Your turn next, Trice. Let's hope you're not such an idiot when it comes to burglary."

"Burglary?" faltered Trice.

"Do you think I'm leaving the country without those emeralds? Face it Trice. Two more days and we'll be making the final delivery; then on to a life of luxury in the sun. The villa, Trice! The pool! Do you think I'm going to be thwarted by those two little goody-goodies?"

Trice gripped the wheel and snorted with excitement. The van leapt forward.

Chapter Four

"What's up Lola?" asked Rachel in the salon next morning.

"The worst has happened," said Lola.

"When Mum saw me on the telly she said she couldn't see my eyes. I've got to have a haircut. Just a very little bit off my fringe please Mrs Morgan."

Lola didn't look too awful, so Rachel agreed to have "a *very* little bit" off her fringe too. That was why she was wrapped in towels when Madam Sizzers arrived.

And it was then, just as she was blowing bits of hair off her nose and looking anxiously in the mirror, that she had a sudden shock. As Lola said afterwards, "it was a moment of divine revelation, like the Oracle at Delphi." "Or like Inspector Morse," said Rachel.

The face of Madam Sizzers was behind her, reflected in the mirror, wearing a strangely triumphant look. Her hand reached out and gripped Rachel's shoulder, hard. The fingernails were red . . . red as blood . . . as blood . . . dipped in blood . . .

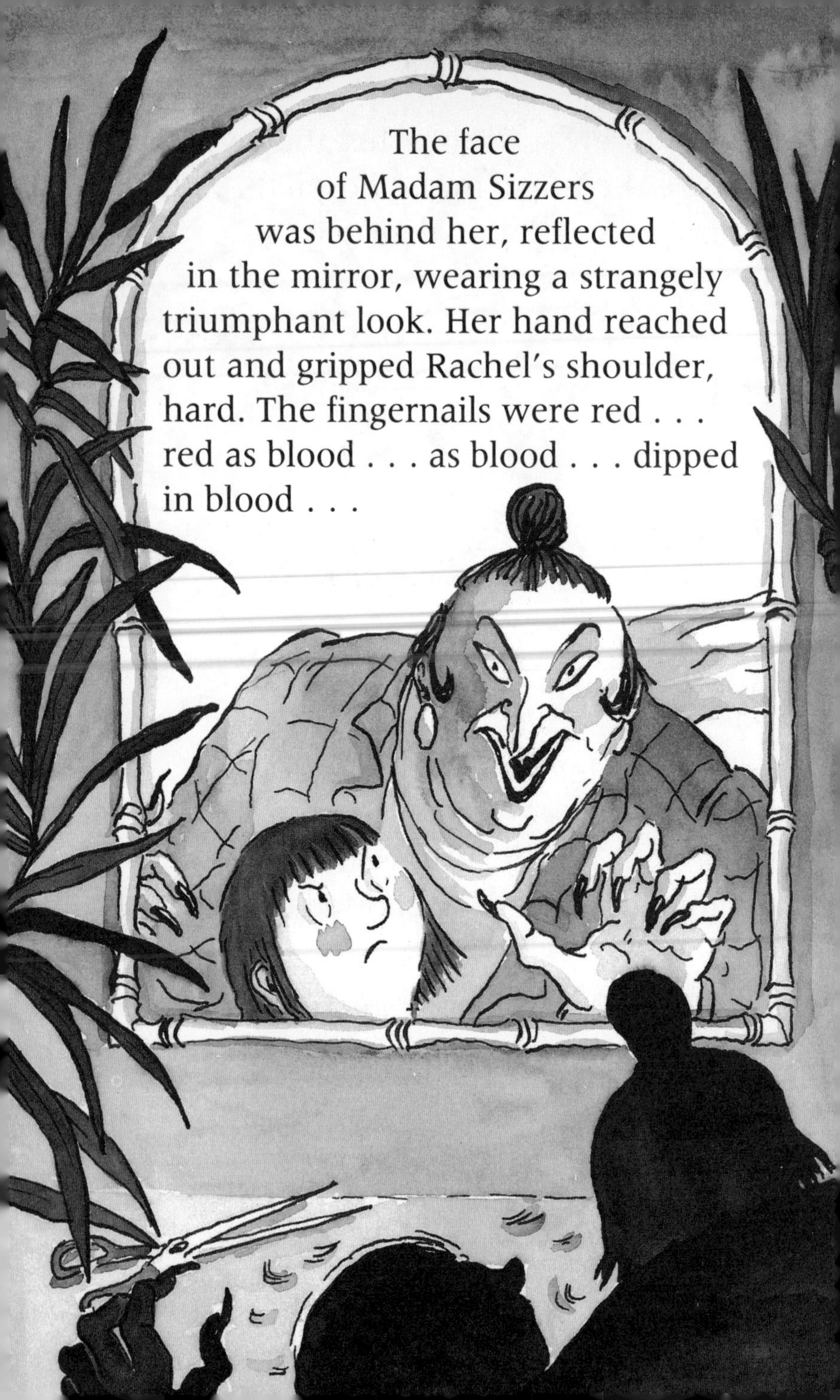

Rachel knew suddenly that they were the nails of the nurse in the hospital . . . nails on the hands that had snatched so frantically for the Lucky Lady necklace!

The gloating face behind her vanished. Beneath the hot wind of the hair dryer, Rachel's brain hummed.

Madam Sizzers! Disguised as a nurse! But why? Why should she go to such lengths, take such risks, to get a necklace anyone could order by post?

Answer: the necklace must be precious, incredibly precious. Perhaps it wasn't the Lucky Lady necklace at all. Perhaps it had been delivered to Rachel by mistake. Perhaps the jewels were real and had been stolen – or smuggled. And Madam Sizzers knew all about it. She was a criminal! A thief!

Rachel's skin prickled all over at the memory of those sharp red nails digging into the soft skin of her neck only seconds ago.

She looked around the salon for Lola. There she sat, writing busily under a twining jasmine, her head wrapped in a towel, her fringe trimmed to eyebrow level.

Rachel got unsteadily to her feet, walked as slowly as she could across the salon, sat down beside Lola, and told her the whole story.

The arm coming through our larder window! That had blood red nails! Dad said so!

"We've got to be really sensible," said Rachel. "We must get the necklace and take it straight to the police station. I'll tell Mum I need something from my bedroom. That's true, after all."

They sauntered casually out of the salon, then began to run as fast as they could to the flats, up the stairs and through the door. They half fell into Rachel's room.

For a moment everything seemed normal. Drawers open, clothes spilling on to the floor, books and comics tossed in heaps beside the bed. But the curtains billowed and blew at the open window and, in the corner, the rug was rolled back above a gaping hole.

Rachel wrung her hands in disbelief.

Lola put her arms around her.

"Don't worry. We'll find them. You look as miserable as a donkey eating thistles."

Rachel tried to laugh. "Yes. Back to Mum. She'll know what to do."

Then she noticed a trickle of earth that trailed across the floor to the window-sill. She rubbed it between her fingers. "That's funny," she thought. "This is just like potting compost."

The eyes of Madam Sizzers glinted as she hid the emerald necklace in her capacious bosom.

"Lucky break, Trice. Haven't forgotten your old tricks, have you?"

She fished in her bag, pulled out a tube of glue, and began to transform her cruel face with a false beard and large black eyebrows.

She passed a blonde wig to Trice.

"Put this on when we're in the van. Drat! I forgot about your moustache. You'll have to shave it off."

"Not flipping likely," said Trice, belligerently.

Chapter Five

How strangely light the salon was. So spacious. And the walls so high and white and empty.

"Where's Madam Sizzers, Mum?" cried Rachel. "And what's happened to the plants?"

But her mother waved her away. She was doing a manicure and concentrating hard.

The hair-washing boy called to them across the salon.

"The man from 'Trice Flowers' came and collected them. He said they needed freshening up. Dunno why. They looked OK to me."

There was a sudden movement by the back door. A man with a drooping moustache was carrying the last spider plant out of the office. A van was revving in the street behind the salon. Rachel and Lola turned and ran out of the front door and round the corner to the rear entrance.

The 'Trice Flowers' van was parked there, its back doors open wide. Inside, it was crammed with pot plants. The man pushed in the spider plant and turned back to the salon. He bent down to lift two huge suitcases.

Without a thought, the two girls ran forward, jumped into the van and crouched behind the plants.

The floor shook as the suitcases skidded towards them and the doors slammed shut.

"What are we doing? We're out of our minds!" hissed Lola despairingly, as the van shuddered, jerked and roared off down the road.

Rachel and Lola huddled miserably on a pile of old sacks at the back of the van. They were bumped and shaken at every turn in the road, and almost overpowered by the sickly scent of tropical flowers.

"I feel like an old, ill chimpanzee in a jungle," moaned Lola. "What can she be doing with all these plants anyway?"

But Rachel was silent. She was thinking hard, thinking of the little trails of earth in the hospital, in her bedroom; earth like potting compost.

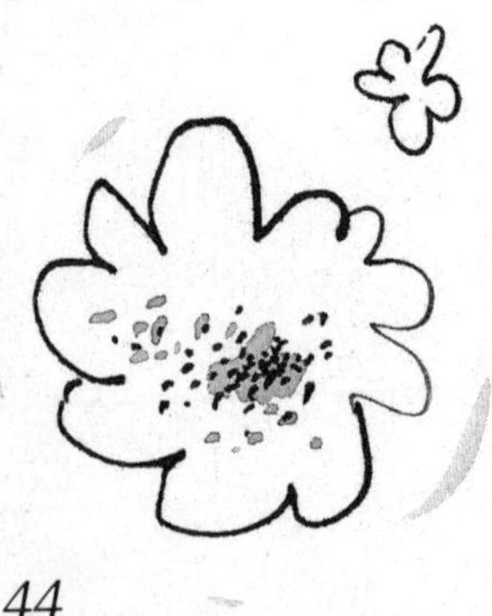

Suddenly she reached for a spider plant and turned it upside down, tipping it out of its pot.

"Rachel! Are you mad?" protested Lola, as earth rained over her legs.

"Look! Look!" hissed Rachel.

At the bottom of the flower pot lay a plastic bag. Inside that was a familiar little leather pouch. Inside that gleamed . . .

Rachel stuffed the spider plant back into the pot and dropped the stones into an empty sack.

"Quick, Lola!"

They began feverishly to up-end every plant in the van. Hidden under every one was a little bag filled with sparkling jewels.

The van swayed wildly, Rachel and Lola were thrown from side to side, but they kept going until every plant was back in its pot, and every bag was in the sack.

"Now what?" said Lola.

The door's locked. We'll just have to wait till they open it, then jump.

They sat hunched against the door, Rachel clutching the sack, as the dusky light outside faded slowly from the sky, and street lamps bathed their tired and anxious faces in a sickly orange glow.

n getaway, eh Trice?" cackled adam Sizzers, her face flushed above the black beard. "Only ten minutes to the airfield. Nothing can stop us now."

Trice was gripping the steering wheel, his knuckles white as bone. "I might have forgotten one small detail," he muttered.

The colour drained from the face of Madam Sizzers. "Yessss?" she hissed.

"Petrol," choked Trice.

Chapter Six

It wasn't the squealing of brakes that woke them, or the juddering halt, but a loud voice, alarmingly close.

"Get on with it, man. We only need two gallons to get to the airfield."

Peering through the rear window, Rachel and Lola watched a strange bearded figure walk under the brilliant lights of the garage forecourt to the payment desk.

"Who's that? Are we in the wrong van, or what?" whispered Lola, completely bewildered.

A lanky woman with a red scarf and long blonde hair was filling the van's petrol tank. A total stranger!

"Madam Sizzers must have escaped," said Rachel in excitement. "Let's get this lady to let us out."

"She could be another accomplice," breathed Lola.

"We'll have to chance it. We can always run."

"Not with my knees like this."

But Rachel knocked boldly on the van window.

The blonde woman
whirled
wildly round,
dropping the
pump nozzle.

Her hands flew
to her face
and she
pressed the
red scarf
over her
mouth.

My... you did give me a fright! What are you naughty girls up to?

Her voice was squeaky. Her hands were shaking as she opened the van door. "Please help us," said Rachel, earnestly. "We must get to a police station straight away."

Of course, my dears. I'll take you there myself. Here comes my friend now. Just stay where you are.

The face of the blonde lady, which had been shadowed, was caught now in the light. The scarf slipped a little. Rachel and Lola gazed, horrified, at the dark moustache drooping from her upper lip.

The bearded man began to run towards them across the forecourt, calling in a high voice, "Slam the door Trice! The door!"

"Jump, Lola! It's Sizzers!" screamed Rachel, and they leapt out together.

"Little swines!" growled Trice, the moustachioed lady, lungeing forward. His feet shot out from under him as he skidded in the pool of petrol.

Rachel and Lola dodged behind the pumps, playing a deadly game of tag, as Madam Sizzers raced towards them.

Forcing every last ounce of strength into their legs, the girls dashed towards the lights of the garage shop, hurled themselves through the swing doors and dived behind the counter.

"Oy, oy! What's up?" cried the cashier.

Madam Sizzers was at the door, leaning there panting, her face twisted into a peculiar, ingratiating smile above the beard.

"Come along now girls. It's past your bedtimes. No more silly games."
Her voice shot higher.
"You bad girls."

But as she spoke, her beard began to slip, slowly, slowly. Rachel, Lola, the cashier and three lorry drivers watched mesmerized as it dropped beneath one ear. With a final furious glance, Madam Sizzers ripped off the beard, flung it to the ground, turned and ran.

In an instant, the tail-lights of the van joined the thousand lights of the motorway and were gone.

Lola sat down suddenly on the floor.

"I told you my knees would give out," she said, shakily.

"Blimey! And I thought I'd seen everything!" said the cashier.

Rachel pressed the buttons on the public phone. Nine. Nine. Nine.

"Emergency services. Fire, police or ambulance?"

"Police," said Rachel, firmly.

A sharp wind cut across the airfield and dark clouds raced past the crescent moon. Waves hurled themselves violently at the rocky shore below.

Trice, his wig askew, clutching his silk scarf around his shoulders, gazed in horror at the spray that hung suspended and shimmering above the cliff top.

Madam Sizzers grunted as she lifted a cheese plant from its pot and reached into the compost.

Eyes narrowing beneath the bushy eyebrows, she pulled out a rubber plant and searched again.

Spider plants, aspidistras, jasmines, hibiscus soon lay scattered at her feet, the earth from the pots drifting along the runway.

"TRICE! THEY'VE GONE! THE JEWELS HAVE GONE!" shrieked Madam Sizzers into the rising wind.

Chapter Seven

Rachel and Lola were allowed to watch from a distance, sitting in a car with a policewoman, high above the airfield.

A single light burned below, beside the hangar, and a small red and white plane was parked beside a green van.

Two figures, one thick-set, the other a slender blonde, stood among a tangle of green plants and broken flowerpots, waving and gesticulating wildly.

They both turned, caught up their suitcases and began to run towards the plane.

At that instant great beams of light blazed at them from around the runway, and scores of dark figures began to race across the tarmac towards them.

"Take a look, lovey," said the policewoman, handing Lola her binoculars.

But she was too late. Sizzers and Trice were surrounded by police. All that could be seen of them now was the golden wig, which lifted from the centre of the crowd, glinted briefly in the searchlights, and was whisked over the cliff top and out to sea on a violent gust of wind.

Everybody in town wanted their hair cut, set or permed that Saturday. Salon Sizzers was packed. Rachel's mum had to get in extra help. Rachel and Lola swept up heaps of hair snippings, handed out rollers, scrubbed out hair-washing basins and told their story a hundred times.

A sign on the desk read "UNDER NEW MANAGEMENT. LYNETTE MORGAN, MANAGERESS."

Outside, a new signboard turned cheerfully in the breeze.
THE LUCKY LADY.
THE LUCKY LADY SALON.

Lola stayed the night at Rachel's, so they could both wake Rachel's mother with her birthday present on Sunday morning.

They sat beside her in bed as she opened the pink tissue paper and lifted out the sparkling necklace.

"Happy Birthday, Mum. It's called 'Sea Foam'. Do you like it?"

"Rachel sent off for it ages ago, but it only arrived yesterday," said Lola.

"I absolutely love it," said Rachel's mum, putting it on over her nightie.